For Milo, from Oupa, with love – *L.B.*

For Catherine and Simon – *S.H.*

Text copyright © 2006 by Louis Baum
Illustrations copyright © 2006 by Sue Hellard

Typeset in Weiss
Art created with watercolor

Published by Bloomsbury Publishing, New York, London, and Berlin
Distributed to the trade by Holtzbrinck Publishers

Library of Congress Cataloging-in-Publication Data
Baum, Louis.
The mouse who braved bedtime / by Louis Baum ; illustrated by Sue Hellard. – 1st U.S. ed.
p.   cm.
Summary: Every night, Milo Mouse has terrible nightmares about a scary monster, but
eventually he confronts his fears, the nightmares stop, and he even makes a new friend.
ISBN-10: 1-58234-691-7 • ISBN-13: 978-1-58234-691-5
[1. Fear–Fiction. 2. Nightmares–Fiction. 3. Monsters–Fiction. 4. Bedtime–Fiction.
5. Mice–Fiction.] I. Hellard, Susan, ill. II. Title.
PZ7.B3269Mo 2006   [E]–dc22   2006014417

First U.S. Edition 2006
Printed in Singapore
1 3 5 7 9 10 8 6 4 2

Bloomsbury Publishing, Children's Books, U.S.A.
175 Fifth Avenue, New York, NY 10010

The Mouse Who Braved Bedtime

by Louis Baum
illustrated by Sue Hellard

BLOOMSBURY
CHILDREN'S
BOOKS

When Milo Mouse woke up in the morning, he felt awful.

"Mom," he said, "I had a scary dream last night. I was so frightened."
"Well," she replied, "maybe it would help if you told me about it."

Milo shivered. "It was dark, and there was a horrible, big scary monster running after me. I couldn't really see the monster, but I knew it had horrible, huge claws."

"Oh, my!" said Mom. "That sounds terrifying!"

"It was," said Milo.

Mom thought for a moment, then said, "I think a nice cup of warm milk just before bedtime will prevent you from having that horrible dream again."

That night, Milo had a nice cup of warm milk just before bedtime.

Then he crept past the dark cupboard under the stairs. Milo hated passing that mysterious door every night. With his heart beating fast, he rushed upstairs to bed.

But when Milo woke up the next morning, he felt even *more* awful.

"Dad, I had a bad dream last night."

"Well, maybe it would help if you told me about it," said Dad.

Milo shivered. "There was a horrible, big scary monster trying to catch me. I couldn't really see it, but the faster I ran, the bigger it got. And I just knew that it had huge, sharp fangs."

"Oh, my!" said Dad. "That doesn't sound very pleasant at all." He thought for a moment, then said, "They say that keeping a window open to let in the fresh air works wonders." So that's what Milo did.

He had a nice cup of warm milk just before bedtime.

Then he crept past the dark cupboard under the stairs . . .

. . . and with his heart beating fast, he rushed upstairs to bed, opened the window, and let in the fresh night air.

But when Milo woke up the next morning,
he felt even *worse* than the day before.

He went straight to his big brother, Jack.

"Jack," he said,
"I had a bad dream last night."
"Well," said Jack, "maybe it would
help if you told me about it."

Milo shivered. "A horrible, big scary monster was trying to catch me. I couldn't really see it, but I knew that if it caught me, it would do horrible things to me. The faster I ran, the bigger the monster got. And I just knew it had big, scary glinting eyes."

"Oh, my!" said Jack. "That does sound pretty horrible."

"It was," said Milo.

Jack thought for a moment, then said, "Try some exercise, Milo. I used to have bad dreams until I started exercising before bedtime."

So that's what Milo did. First, he had a nice cup of warm milk.

Then he crept past the scary cupboard under the stairs, and with his heart beating fast, he rushed upstairs to bed.

He opened the window to let in the fresh night air.

And then he did twelve exercises.

But when Milo woke up the next morning, he had *never* felt worse. And he felt awful all day because now he had no one else to ask for help.

Before he went to bed that night, he had a nice cup of warm milk. But instead of rushing upstairs, he stopped and turned.

A light had been left on in the cupboard.

"I wonder what's in there," thought Milo. With his body trembling all over, he peeked inside.

Inside the cupboard were blankets, sheets,
pillowcases, and some big fluffy bath towels.
"Oh," said Milo, trembling a bit less.
"Sheets and towels are nothing to be afraid of."

Then Milo climbed upstairs and left the window open really wide to let in the fresh night air.

He did fifteen exercises.

Then Milo got into bed and lay awake a long, long time. The last thing he wanted was to fall asleep and meet that horrible scary monster again. Milo thought of many things. He thought about the monster . . .

and his claws . . .

and his fangs . . .

He thought about the monster's horrible, horrible growls coming closer and closer.

Then he thought about how he had braved the cupboard under the stairs. Really, there had been nothing to worry about.

And as he fell asleep, Milo had a smile on his face.

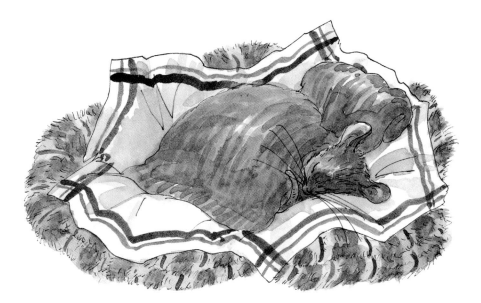

But Milo's dream was dark and scary. He ran as fast as he could, but something was running behind him. The faster Milo ran, the faster the thing behind him ran as well!

Milo's heart was beating fast, and he tried to run faster, but he was getting out of breath. His little paws felt heavy, he felt very tired, and he knew that whatever was behind him was quickly catching up.

Suddenly Milo remembered that the dark
cupboard under the stairs was filled only with
sheets, pillowcases, and big fluffy bath towels.
So Milo stopped.
And the thing behind him stopped.
Milo turned around.

Milo woke up with a start. Sitting on his bed was a field mouse, just half his size.

"Who are you?" demanded Milo.

"I'm Logan," said the field mouse. "I sleep in that little matchbox on the windowsill. Every night, I've been trying to wake you up to play."

"I thought you were a horrible scary monster," said Milo.

"*Me*, a horrible scary monster?" said Logan. "Don't make me laugh." And he laughed. Milo laughed too.

"Can we be friends?" Logan asked.

Milo thought for a minute. "That sounds like a good idea. Yes. Let's be friends."

So they were. And they played lots of games together. But the game they liked playing most was . . .

scary
monsters!